THE MOM COMS

PROLOGUE

BRITTANEE NICOLE   JENNI BARA   SWATI M.H.
DAPHNE ELLIOT

MOM Coms

Four best friends, seven kids, one falling down Boston brownstone, and a pact to stay together forever.

What could possibly go wrong?

Mother Faker
By Brittanee Nicole

Mother Maker
By Jenni Bara

Mother Pucker
By Swati M.H.

Mother Hater
By Daphne Elliot

PREORDER THE SERIES ON AMAZON

Liv

Deep breaths.

In, one, two, three...

Out, one, two, three.

"Liv, are you listening to me?" my boss asks over the phone as I stare down at my luggage, then dart my gaze to my future ex-husband. He's covered in glitter from head to toe, and his face is beet red. Beside him, my four year old son Finn stands with his head down, Nerf gun in hand, tutu around his waist, and tears streaming down his face. My youngest daughter Adeline squeals in delight as she picks up the glitter from the floor and tosses it over her head. At two years old, glitter is magical, but for my forty year old husband...? Yeah, not so much.

"Liv," Beckett growls into the phone, his patience waning.

I swallow and snap into action, pulling Finn from Drake's death grip and turning him away so he doesn't see the disap-pointment his father so easily wears on his face. Drake has little patience for Finn–something he has in common with my boss. They are both ready to snap.

As I run a soothing hand against Finn's hair, quieting him immediately, I speak into the phone. "Mr. Langfield, I'm off for the next three days. Sara is available. I'll call her as soon as we get off the phone and make sure she's there for the meetings."

He groans into the phone and my eyes dart to my husband, who leers at me as he swipes glitter from his suit.

Any minute now, my best friend Dylan will be here so we can leave for our annual girls trip. I *need* this trip. Hell, it's a miracle I convinced my husband to watch his own children just so I could escape for a few days. I haven't even taken a day off from work since my last girls trip, and my boss–of all people–is *not* ruining this for me.

"That won't do," Beckett says into the phone. "Cancel your plans."

"I can't cancel my plans," I say slowly as Drake snaps his gaze at me triumphantly. I can already see the wheels spinning in his head. He thinks if I don't go away, then he doesn't have to help with the kids. He's already staring at the door, planning his own escape.

"Liv, this is a twenty-million-dollar deal we are talking about. I need you there."

"And I need a break," I whisper into the phone, emotion getting the best of me.

"It's in the Keys, Liv. You'll have plenty of time to relax."

My son places one chubby hand on my cheek and frowns at me sadly. "I'm sorry, Mama. I won't shoot glitter again."

I'd laugh if I didn't feel like sobbing. My son loves Nerf guns . . . and glitter. I just never thought he'd combine the two. Our house and the sparkles that will likely never come out of the rug are a prime example of how wrong I was about that. And my husband's hair. That actually does make me want to laugh.

He's balding in the back, so from behind, his head shines with the additional sparkles. I sink my head against my son's and mouth, "It's okay, buddy. Go get cleaned up, and I'll be up to say goodbye."

I set him in the direction of his room, and then say to my boss, "My friends all took the weekend off. We booked a suite in San Francisco; we have tours set for wineries and spa services, and I can't just not show up."

"So bring them," he says nonchalantly, like it's no big deal to change plans at the drop of a hat.

"Beckett," I sigh, knowing he won't stop until he gets his way, "we have plane tickets. I can't. Just have Sara go with you."

"Your friends can come on the jet with us. Please, Liv, I really need you."

Despite the fact that I work for Langfield Corp., and not just the Boston Revs–the baseball team he owns–Beckett seems to think I'm his personal assistant and not the head of PR. He always *needs* me for something.

I groan. "I'll see what I can do."

I hang up and turn my attention to Drake. Before I leave, I need to make sure he's not going to make Finn feel any worse than he already does.

"It was an accident," I start.

Drake glares as he swipes a hand over his head and glitter rains down on him. I pull my lips together to keep from laughing. "Liv, this isn't working," he says as his eyes narrow at my folded lips.

I roll my eyes at his dramatics and reach down to pick up Adeline. She gives me a big toothy grin and swipes her hands in my hair, giving me a little extra sparkle. "As much as I'd love to discuss this, Dylan will be here any minute, and I now have to figure out a way to convince my friends to ditch our original trip and come with me to the Keys."

"No. What you need to figure out is how you're going to get a new job. I'm not living like this anymore."

A hiss sounds from above us, and I look up in time to watch as one of the glitter blobs—which was once a silicone playtoy filled with gel and glitter, a sensory toy that belonged to my oldest daughter, Winnie—detach from the ceiling. Finn had shot it right before he launched a glitter bomb at his father. Hopefully, it was last week that Winnie needed glitter for her art project, and not Monday.

It happens slowly, the blob peeling off the ceiling one millimeter at a time. Drake looks up just as it detaches from the ceiling, and then it's almost like the entire event occurs in slow motion. The blob spins, the goo inside sliding back and forth, and then, with a *splat*, it breaks open right as it hits him in the face, the glittery goo sliding down and mixing with the rest of the glitter he's coated in.

I laugh. It's not funny–none of this is particularly funny–but I really don't know what else to do. Drake told me last week he's moving out. He said he'd do me this one last favor of watching our children while I go away, but after that, he's done. I work fifty hours a week, if I'm lucky, though most of the time it's closer to sixty. The Langfield Group owns Boston's sports, so my weekends are spent between hockey and baseball games— evenings spent by Beckett Langfield's side as he woos sponsors and players—making sure he doesn't say something that offends someone.

I fail at that job almost daily.

We hired a nanny to help out with the children, and my husband went and fell for her. So now I don't have a nanny or a husband. Honestly, I'd prefer the nanny, but I draw my line at begging women who sleep with my husband to help me.

Basically, my life is a shit show, and I just need seventy-two hours with my three besties to regroup and figure out how the hell I am going to keep my job and parent my children without the help of a spouse. Living in Boston isn't cheap, and neither is full-time help.

So I laugh as Drake swipes the glittering goo off his face, and I laugh as he grimaces because he's got some in his mouth. Then I take three deep breaths, straighten my shoulders, and stand up to the asshole who looks like an art project gone wrong. "Seventy-two hours, Drake. You promised me seventy-two hours. Call Kendall if you need help. And if you yell at our son over his choice of clothes, I'll castrate you."

Drake clenches his fists but he doesn't say another word. When the doorbell chimes, I kiss our daughter, then hand her off before I make my way to the front door.

Vacation, here we come.

* * *

"I mean, can you believe this?" Dylan asks, her gold eyes bouncing between me and the private plane we're currently sitting on.

My boss flicks his eyes toward us, his gaze narrowed. She's definitely too happy for his liking. Well, too fucking bad. He's the one who interrupted our perfectly planned weekend.

I accept the champagne the stewardess offers and clink my glass against Dylan's outstretched one. "To the universe providing this amazing plane," Dylan cheers as I take a sip.

I stifle a giggle. "It's not the universe, Dyl; it's my demanding boss."

Beckett glowers at me, and I shrug as I take another sip. No one dares to piss off Beckett Langfield—he fires people for just looking at him wrong.

Normally, I avoid pissing him off, too, but apparently, alcohol makes me brave.

"Your boss may have been the one who provided us with

the plane," she explains as if she's teaching a toddler her ABCs, "but it was the universe which set it all in motion."

"Well, if you could ask the universe to provide a full-time nanny–one who doesn't screw my husband–a forty-hour work week, and a weekly orgasm, I'd much appreciate it," I retort, tipping my glass in her direction.

Dylan's eyes grow wide. "Drake cheated?"

I sigh as I settle back against the soft leather seats. This plane is actually really nice, and it's not my first time on it, either. "Promise you won't tell the girls. I don't want to ruin our fun trip with my drama," I whisper, then quietly fill her in on exactly how bad the drama has gotten between Drake and me.

The last thing I want is my boss to know about my disaster of a life. Beckett doesn't do drama... or people. And he definitely doesn't want to hear about my childcare problems. Basically, he's a robot who makes time for nothing but his friends and work.

And I'm sure there is the occasional orgasm in there for him. *Although, knowing him, he probably schedules that, too.*

I giggle at the thought.

Or maybe it's the champagne bubbles tickling my throat.

"Why are you laughing?" Dylan whispers.

"I'm picturing my boss having sex," I admit, and then the giggles really take over.

Dylan glances in his direction, her long auburn hair swaying as she does, then, without her lips moving, she replies, "I'd imagine only missionary. Maybe three thrusts and then a grunt as he comes."

I spit out my champagne. Dylan mastered the art of talking like a ventriloquist sometime in college, and she'd drive our teachers crazy, blurting things out at the most inopportune times, and then they'd be looking all over the room in search of the culprit.

She's the fun to my quiet, the crazy to my boring. But somehow, whenever I'm around her, I don't *feel* boring or straightlaced. It's like she brings out the best in me, and for seventy-two hours, I'm happy I get to be *this* version of me.

Even if I get fired in the process. Who am I kidding? The man needs me. No one else could deal with Beckett Langfield, and he knows it.

The stewardess appears with a napkin, which I use to clean up the champagne I've sprayed my lap with. Then I blot at the tears, which are still streaming down my face from laughing so hard. "God, I'd take missionary," I whisper.

"With him?" she says far too loudly.

Beckett lifts his head again and when his green eyes connect with mine, I almost feel it in my bones. His stare dares me to answer her honestly, but I look away and nudge Dylan. "No. New topic."

But even as the conversation turns to a story about Dylan's son and the crazy antics he's gotten into, my body continues to burn. Glancing back at my boss, I watch as he sips his Hanson whiskey as he studies the paper in front of him–likely stats for the player we're trying to acquire this weekend. He runs his hand through his dark brown locks. Unlike Drake, he's been blessed in the hair department.

It's full and would probably be fun to tug on during sex . . .

Where the hell did that thought just come from?

I shake myself out of the daze, reminding myself that I'm a single mom with three kids under the age of eight, with hips the size of probably two of the women he'd normally date, and with no time for anything but work and my kids.

Beckett Langfield will never be anything more to me than a pain in my ass, and not the fun kind.

Shayla

"Remember, we're not crazy nuts, we're healthy nuts!" I repeat our slogan to my eight-year-old with as much enthusiasm as I can muster.

He's more perceptive than I give him credit for, and I'm hoping my over-the-top bright smile that rivals the sun veils the panic in my voice.

"I remember, Mom." His chestnut brown eyes study me as I kneel in front of him with his small hands inside of mine. "I'm going to be fin–"

I tighten my hands on his wrist, trying to assert how important it is that he understands what I'm about to say. "Remember to brush your teeth with the charcoal toothpaste twice every day. Oh, and I've put your organic vitamins in the daily pill-boxes." He already knows this because he's used to our routine, but it can never hurt to remind him again. "And remember to double-knot your shoelaces." I look down at the offending laces tied in bunny ears with a frown before looking back up. "I wish you'd stuck to wearing velcro shoes. At least I wouldn't have to worry about you tripping and falling and cracking your head open."

"I'm eight, Mom, not three." He looks so much like Ajay when he grimaces–the same downturned eyes and thinned lips, the same square jaw and thick dark hair. One day he's going to be a knockout just like his dad was, and I can't decide if that brings me more heartache than joy.

I'm sure Ajay is smiling down on him right now from his massage chair in heaven, watching his son fight me for more independence each day.

But, so help me God, I will fight him on this shoelaces-versus-velcro war for as long as I can. So what if he's a forty-five-year-old man wearing velcro shoes? At least he'll be safe.

I pull my son to my chest again, holding his small frame against me. "I'm going to miss you so much. Remember, I'm only a phone call away. You can FaceTime me anytime you want." At his nod, I quickly amend my words. "But also, screens aren't good for your eyes, so we can't video call for too long, either. And only one hour of screen time after dinner, okay?"

My son's shoulders slump. He's always been a quiet kid but after Ajay died, he's become even more introverted. "Okay, Mom." He sighs. "You don't have to worry so much."

I can understand how annoying I must sound to him. I never thought I'd become this overbearing, nagging mother, either, but loss does strange things to a person. So much of my life is tied to this sweet boy standing in front of me because he's really all I have left. And as much as I try to take care of him, he doesn't realize that he's the only thing keeping me together most days.

I nod vigorously to agree with him, but really, it's more to convince myself. He's going to be fine. *Totally fine!* It's only for a few days, and despite my stepmom's *interesting* personality, he's in good hands.

I glance through the window in the front door at the black SUV with dark-tinted windows and a driver wearing a suit that likely costs more than my monthly mortgage here in San Francisco. It seems a little overkill to be chauffeured to the airport in such luxury, but Liv's boss, Beckett Langfield, insisted. And apparently, whatever Beckett Langfield insists upon, Beckett Langfield gets.

I just wish he had a modicum of regard for our environment. There is absolutely no need to pollute the air further by having a behemoth like that carting one person around. Well, more like five people, if I consider the bulk of the large man still waiting for me outside.

Had I known this was the car he was going to send, I would have taken my Prius and just parked at the airport.

My three best friends and I were supposed to be going on our yearly girls trip this weekend, but what was supposed to be a wine country getaway morphed into a cross-country flight to the Florida Keys to Beckett Langfield's multi-million-dollar estate.

Why? Again, because he *insisted* that Liv work through the weekend–on her scheduled vacation, no less–and, because he's the owner of the Boston Revs baseball team. I recall Liv telling me that his family owns Kai's–and my late husband's–favorite hockey team, the Boston Bolts, too.

I won't be telling Kai whose house I'm staying at, of course. He'd go nuts, *and not the healthy kind.* He'd wind up asking me a million questions, which would inevitably turn into our daily argument–ahem, *discussion*–about him wanting to learn hockey.

Anyway, I digress.

I suppose there are worse things to complain about than spending time in a billionaire's home. If I didn't worry about

Kai as much, I might feel better about the whole situation, but as it is, I'm a ball of nerves.

Speaking of balls and nerves, I'm still irritated that my travel-sized toy didn't come in on time. Unfortunately, I had to pack my big wand last minute.

A girl's gotta do what a girl's gotta do. And if that means a girl's gotta do herself . . . well, then so be it.

I'm just about to remind Kai about his eight PM sleep schedule and his daily nasal rinse when my stepmom comes bounding down the stairs.

She got in late last night from Arizona but thankfully, I was able to go through the entire safety and wellbeing checklist twice with her then, and once this morning.

"Ah, you're still here," she says almost exhaustedly, giving me a small smile along with a slow blink from under her teal cat-eye glasses. They match her solid teal dress and offset from the curly white wig, reminiscent of Betty White.

Since the day I met her at the age of twelve when my widower father introduced me to her, Merna, my stepmother, has always changed her entire outfit *daily*. And by entire outfit, I mean, hair, nail color, and makeup, apart from just her clothes. And what better to give her hair a nice change than a new wig! At this point, I'd be hard-pressed to guess her real hair color or style.

Nevertheless, as strange as she might appear on the outside, she's a gem on the inside and loves me and my son dearly. So, if that love comes with a little bit of eccentricism on her part, then I don't have any complaints about it.

"I'm leaving. I promise." I rise to my feet and lean in to plant a kiss on her cheek. "I was just reminding Kai about–"

"Shayla." Merna places her hands on my shoulders and gives me a pointed look from below those glasses again. "I've got it. He will eat only organic, home-cooked meals with reduced salt and no sugar. He will watch no more than an hour of TV each day and will instead go on long walks with me. I'll also make sure he sleeps on time and brushes his teeth at least twice a day."

"With the charcoal toothpaste," I add with emphasis. *Maybe I should pull up the safety and wellbeing checklist again . . .* From my recollection of my own childhood, Merna *was* somewhat lackadaisical about schedules and rules.

She purses her lips. "With the *charcoal* toothpaste."

My eyes flick from my stepmom to my son, and seeing his sullen face, I lift up his chin. "Hey, I'll be back soon. Plus, it's not like you won't eat anything fun. I baked those sweet potato brownies you love so much!"

His frown deepens. "Can I go swimming with *Nani*?" He refers to my stepmom.

My body tenses and I shove back the thoughts of him possibly drowning. "No, honey. We've talked about this, remember? The only activity I'm okay with is walking or jogging at a steady pace in a well-lit park. There are too many kids who drown every–"

"Oh, look!" my stepmom says animatedly. "That driver, dressed like *Dwayne, The Rock, Johnson,* seems to have waited long enough for you. You've got to get going or you'll be late, Shay." She shuffles me toward the door with her hand on my bicep. "Now, off you go before you miss your flight."

"But–" I try to interject as she literally pushes me through my front door.

"You don't worry about a thing. He's my grandson, and I will take care of him."

"But maybe we could go through the safety and wellbeing check–"

Merna starts to close the door on my face. "Have a

wonderful time with your friends, sweetheart. Love you. Bye now!"

And a second later, I'm looking at my red-painted front door, wondering if I've made the right decision.

* * *

The light from the moon illuminates the ink-colored waves before they crash into a blanket of white foam a few feet from where I sit.

Despite the fact that I flew first class for the first time in my life, the flights were delayed in Atlanta due to the weather, so my ten-hour journey became more like fourteen. By the time I got into the ridiculously lavish paradise that Beckett Langfield calls a mere vacation home, it was well past one AM. I was so exhausted, even the plush mattress didn't help. And after what happened at the airport, I could barely stand to look at my wand without flushing at the thought.

So, instead of tossing this way and that in bed, I decided to take a walk on the beach, letting the salty scent and spray from the ocean relax me from the outside in.

I look along the stretch of dark sand, noting there's not a person in sight. It's a little unnerving at this hour, but the crashing waves provide a good distraction to the quiet.

I shift on my side and pull out the box I avoided reaching for all last week, but now I'm jonesing hard. "Just one," I tell myself. "One and then you're done."

The weight and sight of it in my hand disgusts me. It goes against everything I stand for, everything I teach and value. I'm a physical therapist, for fuck's sake! I lost my husband just two years ago to cancer! What the hell am I doing jonesing for a smoke like a street junkie? I should be ashamed of myself.

And even though the salty breeze overpowers everything in its way, the scent of tobacco and mint linger in my nose.

Beseeching. Coercing. *Just one.*

I justify it.

Of course, I do.

I mean, I literally ate nothing but quinoa and spinach today. My daily meals consist of a kale and banana smoothie with turmeric and chia seeds on Mondays, Wednesdays, and Fridays and organic chicken salad with dates, cottage cheese, and fenugreek on the other days. I can afford *one* little cigarette, can't I?

What would Ajay say?

I swallow, twirling the little tobacco-filled tube between my fingers.

He'd understand. He'd have to understand.

It's been . . . it's been hard without him. It hasn't been fair. Nothing has been fair. And if he had anything to say about the way I'm coping, well . . . then he should have been here to say it! He shouldn't have left me here on my own. I shouldn't have to deal with everything alone.

Putting the stick between my lips and placing the box on the sand next to me, I cup my hands over the lighter to ward off the breeze enough to spark the end. I take a long drag, letting the smoke float through my throat and into my lungs–

"Oh, Jesus!" I practically jump out of my skin when I see someone sitting *right fucking next to me.*

Dylan–one of my best friends–stares at me blankly from her spot. By the time I got in, I assumed everyone else was asleep, so I tried to be quiet as I snuck over to the beach. Clearly, my somewhat crazy and deceptively astute best friend– with the million-colored beads around her wrists and wavy auburn hair–has found me.

I quickly throw the offending white stick into the edge of the wave brushing my toes and press my thigh over the box on the sand.

"What the hell, Dyl!" I squeal, trying to lower my heart rate. "When did you get here? I didn't even hear you."

She looks out into the ocean and shrugs–*shrugs!*–after practically making my heart stop. "Just now. The universe wanted me to find you, so it led me here."

I place a hand over my chest, my heart still pounding against it. "Did the universe also tell you to give me a heart attack? Jesus, woman!"

She smiles, her amber eyes swimming in mirth. "No, it's not your time yet. Although your aura is saying a lot, it's not screaming heart attack."

Since the day we met in college, Dylan has been all about reading the signs from the universe and letting the stars lead her through life. And though she had to drop out early because she got pregnant with her son, Liam, we only grew closer through the years.

She's always been the glue between all of us–getting us all talking on the group chats, ensuring we meet up for girls trips, supporting us no matter the physical distance.

I turn and pull her into me, giving her a hug. "I'm so glad to see you."

"Me, too," she whispers, tightening her arms around me. "I missed you."

"Same," I say, pulling away, and then remember what she saw. I quickly stuff the white cigarette box into the pocket of my shorts and clear my throat. "Um . . . it's not what it looked like."

Dylan raises her brows. "No, nothing ever really is. That's the weird thing about eyes; they get so much wrong."

"I wasn't smoking if that's what you were thinking."

"I wasn't." A strand of her hair flies in the breeze and she drags it behind her ear. "I'm pretty sure I saw you with one of those light-up whistles."

I purse my lips, barely able to contain my smile. I've always loved how non-judgmental she is. "That's exactly what it was. A light-up whistle."

"I'm pretty sure I saw you 'light up a whistle' in college too, when you were really stressed."

I grin. "Are we talking about whistles, cigarettes, or dicks? The analogy is interchangeable."

"Definitely dicks," she says, grinning back.

I laugh before we sit in silence for a moment, enjoying the salty ocean spray against our skin.

"How was your flight?" Dylan asks, just as I'm about to start thinking about Kai again. I hope he ate all his vegetables and brushed his teeth before bed. I need to call him in the morning.

I glance at her before looking back at the waves. "I'm pretty sure I'm on some TSA watch list now."

"What?" She swings her head toward me, but I can hear the giggle in her voice even before she speaks. "What happened?"

Running a hand over my face, I tuck the short strands of my asymmetrical bob behind my ear. "I ordered a travel vibrator but it didn't get in on time, so I had to bring my other one."

Her eyes grow into saucers. "Like a big one? The wand?"

I nod, recalling the TSA agent's face when he pulled my heavy *Magic Wand* out of my suitcase and handed it to me to turn off.

"Ma'am. Please turn off your, uh . . . personal massager."

I looked around frantically, noticing an older gentleman in a suit, waiting for his luggage to come through the conveyor belt, giving me and my wand the side-eye. There was also a woman around thirty-five, like me, who tried to bite back her smile. And yet another woman who pulled her school-aged daughter by the arm toward her, as if to create distance from me and my evil toy. As if at any moment, I would hold her daughter hostage with a vibrating dildo to her head.

"It's . . . it's for a friend. She has back problems and this . . . works

well." I managed to string some words together, feeling my cheeks light on fire.

I grabbed the vibrating massager from his gloved hand and turned it off.

Except, instead of turning it off, I accidentally pressed the button to make it buzz louder and faster. My hand shook as the vibration went up my arm. Panicking, I pressed a couple more buttons before finally turning it off.

I stared at the TSA agent's expressionless face as he watched my debacle before squaring my shoulders and holding my head high. "In case you're wondering, personal massagers can be of utmost use as sleep aids and in managing stress."

I shoved the wand back into my suitcase before zipping it up. "Not to mention, they're good for vaginal health." And just to make my point clear, I added with a jab to the air, "I, for one, have exceptional vaginal health!"

And with that, I set my sights toward my gate and rolled my suitcase behind me, paying little mind to the snickering at my back.

Dylan is in a fit of giggles by the time I finish the story, wiping her tears with the back of her hand. "Only you would turn an embarrassing situation into a medical information session."

When we've both caught our breaths from laughing, she puts a hand over my wrist and I turn toward her. "Are you okay? You're clearly not sleeping and . . ." She glances at my pocket where she knows I've stashed the cigarette box. "Well, you're lighting up whistles again."

I know she's trying to make light of what she saw, but she deserves my honesty. She's only ever been honest with me, and I know how much she cares.

I sigh, looking back at the ocean. "I don't know, Dyl. Sometimes my life just feels like it's unraveling. Like I have nothing holding all my pieces together, except Kai. And that's a huge burden to put on an eight-year-old."

I think about Kai and my life in California. We've finally found our new normal after Ajay's death. But is it anything like I envisioned for myself? No.

It's lonely. A life where the only things that keep me company, besides my son, are the memories of the greatest love of my life. A love that you only get once in a lifetime.

I know Kai is not happy, either. Aside from the fact that he misses his dad–his best friend–he doesn't have any friends. It doesn't help that I don't let him do normal things like other kids do, but I just *can't*. The prospect of him getting hurt or worse . . .

No, I refuse to even let that thought creep back into my head.

Dylan hums, nodding. "I get that. But, Shay, you're forgetting something else in your arsenal, at your disposal, to hold you all together."

My brows pinch. "What's that?"

"Your strength, your courage, and most importantly," her amber eyes gleam, "*us*, your best friends."

Delia

"Mom." I sigh into the phone. From the second I picked up, she's been completely frazzled. God bless my mom, she is very loving, but not super capable. "I'm sure it's fine."

"I cracked," she says, and I can hear her chewing her nails over the phone. "I just threw the tablets at them. I ran out of ideas."

I take a deep breath, trying to sound soothing. "You got this, Mom."

"I had no choice." Her voice wavers. "We went sailing where they corrected the captain's knot tying skills, then it was off to the beach, home for piano and Zooming with the math tutor, and that puzzle you brought, the one with 5,000 pieces? Already assembled on the dining room table."

"You've had a busy day." I say without a hint of sympathy. *Welcome to my world.* Where I do all of this, plus work seventy hours a week, travel internationally, and lick the boots of my partner overlords at Burns & Glen daily.

Correction: used to.

Not strictly employed at the moment, but even Mom doesn't know that yet. When you're known for being the uptight perfectionist who crushes every goal she sets her sights on, it's kind of hard to admit you had a breakdown at your law firm, called the managing partner a spineless cocksucker, and dramatically quit–and that was all before breaking a heel on your $1,200 Louboutins and falling directly on your face.

The gossip about me is rampant in legal circles, but my mother lives a very tranquil and stress-free existence in the small town of Havenport, MA. She has a little oceanfront bungalow, which I bought for her after *he-who-must-not-be-named* left her penniless, and she's working through her issues with her very pricey therapist–which I also pay for.

And one weekend per year–*one weekend*–I ask her to watch the girls. And invariably, it becomes a screen-time and sugar fest, and I have to spend the next two weeks detoxing them, sending her flowers, and repairing all the damage to her house.

"Mom, you raised me; they are just mini versions."

She laughs. "Delia. Lord knows you were a difficult child." Snort. "But these little hellions are ten times more clever than you ever were, and they have even less impulse control."

"I appreciate you so much," I say through gritted teeth. This trip is almost over, and I just want to get my blood pressure down for an hour before I fly back to Boston and to the shit-show that is my life at the moment.

"Can I say goodnight?" I ask gently.

I hear some shuffling in the background and then Phoebe answers. "Get your sister and put me on speaker," I say firmly. With the twins, you can never show any weakness.

"We're here," they singsong in the cutest possible way.

"Girls. You promised you would cooperate at Grandma's

house." Am I pleading with my eight-year-old twins? Why yes, yes I am.

"It's so boring here," Phoebe whispers. "She got us Play-Doh, Mommy... like we're babies."

I squeeze my eyes shut and pinch the bridge of my nose. "Okay. Grandma said she gave you your tablets. If you brush your teeth and get ready for bed, you can each have thirty minutes. I set the parental controls before I left."

"Mommy, we can disable those faster than you could blink!" I hear Collette giggle in the background. "We just use a proxy server and then clear the browsing history." I look around for a wall to bang my head against.

If I had a time machine, I would go back in time and choose a different sperm donor. Instead of the MIT graduate and former Olympic rower I paid top-dollar for, I should have gone more run-of-the-mill. An accountant? Or even better, a contractor or carpenter. Some sweet dumbass whose only job is to hammer nails. That would be nice...

It had seemed like such a good idea at the time, to fulfill my dream of motherhood without having to deal with complications of the male variety. And I had the resources. So off to Boston's most elite sperm bank I went, and between that super seed and my own overachieving eggs, I may have inadvertently produced a duo who could bring about the end of days.

Phoebe and Collette weren't just smart. They could read at three, and now spoke fluent French, but they had also been born with the unshakable inclination to always use their powers for evil instead of good.

After saying goodnight and extracting a promise not to psychologically torture their grandmother in exchange for ice cream, a movie night, and new coding software, I got off the phone, desperate for some girl time.

Looking to top off my wine, I made my way through the kitchen. I was itchy and tired and not relaxing even a tiny bit.

We had already been here a full twenty-four hours, and I was doing an amazing job of faking it with my friends. I had perfected the alpha bitch act in preschool, so I was well-practiced at projecting the image of having my shit together.

It's not that I want to lie. These three women are my ride or dies. After becoming suitemates our freshman year of college, we've been inseparable for the last seventeen years. There have been ups and downs and really hard days, but we are always there for one another. And these beautiful, enduring friendships are some of the most precious things in my life.

And here we are, on our annual girls weekend–and I was sneaking off every few hours to cry in my bedroom. Thank God I'd come stocked with my La Mer eye cream because this was nuclear-level puffiness that not even my finest YSL concealer could fix.

In fairness, I had expected to be drowning my sorrows in some fine vintages during our winery tour, but somehow, we had ended up on a private island off the coast of Florida instead because some bossy billionaire hijacked our girls trip. It's just like a man to try to control women's bodies . . .

Sadly, everyone else has gone to bed, leaving me with only my thoughts for company. And wine. Always wine.

I make my way through the cavernous kitchen, where some helpful staff member set up a charcuterie spread the size of a midsize sedan on the center island.

"Having fun, Cordelia?"

I turn and find Beckett sitting by the large bay window that looks out at the ocean with a glass of whiskey and a laptop in front of him.

My eyes narrow. I dislike him deeply. Not just because of

what he represents, but because of the way he treated Liv. She's always a pleaser and one of the kindest soul to walk the earth. A lot of people out there take advantage of it–namely, her dumbass husband and her narcissist boss. I've been protecting her like a rabid bulldog for more than a decade and have no plans to stop anytime soon.

"You can let the poor woman just live her life, you know?" I say, ignoring his question. "We'd all be having a lot more fun if she didn't have to be at your beck and call throughout our one yearly girls weekend."

"I'm so sorry you're not enjoying your free *luxury* vacation." He sneers. His attractiveness makes him more abhorrent. If you're going to be a soulless billionaire, then you could at least be short and ugly, with some kind of inoperable goiter and a raging case of male pattern baldness. The tall, dark, and handsome bullshit only makes his existence more offensive.

"Oh please." I pour what is likely a $1,000 bottle of wine into my thirty-two-ounce Yeti tumbler. "This costs you nothing, and actually, you're making money because you have your minion here to do your bidding."

"Liv is well-compensated," he grumbles into his glass.

"Keep telling yourself that when you make her cancel her vacations." I start to walk away, but turn around. "Do me a favor? Keep being terrible. Because I cannot wait to sue your ass. It will bring me such joy to take your money and fuck with your reputation, exposing you as the narcissistic daddy's boy assburger I know you really are."

He raises his glass to me, the lines around his eyes crinkling. "Always a pleasure, Cordelia."

I raised my tumbler full of wine. "Billionaires shouldn't exist. Eat the rich."

"Says the woman carrying a Chanel purse," he scoffs.

"Fuck off. It was a *gift*."

"Sure thing. You're a real woman of the people."

"Have a terrible night, asshole."

"Sweet dreams, Medusa."

I stride out of the kitchen with extra venom coursing through my veins. I had lied; I bought this bag after my first trial. A huge moment for me, one I thought was the start of something incredible. Sadly, things did not turn out that way.

I look at my gorgeous quilted purse as I make my way out the back door. This was its last hurrah. I'll be selling it once I get back to Boston–along with all my designer clothes, bags, shoes, and my Audi. Since I am no longer on the partner track at Burns & Glen and I have no trust fund to fall back on. My dipshit father had made sure of that. But my fall from grace won't break me. Instead I'll figure something out. Because my girls, both my daughters and my friends, need me to be strong.

My fingers enjoyed the feel of the leather and the chain strap. Returning to my room, I lovingly place it on the bed before heading out to the beach to clear my head.

I decide to walk a little farther, away from the compound, hoping the silence will calm my nerves. Who am I if I'm not some ass kicking lawyer? And why is it so hard to just get everything done every day?

Deep down, I knew the answer. Because society lied to us. As women, we were told we could have it all, do all the things well every day. But you know what? That's a crock of shit.

And I was prepared to give things up. I knew I couldn't have a successful relationship, kids, and a great career, so I cut out the husband part and focused on the career and kids, hoping for two out of three.

But right now, I'm failing at everything.

How will I support my kids? My name is mud in the legal world. Because elite law firms require one thing and one thing alone, *discretion*. If we're going to serve our clients and keep their secrets, then we must be self-controlled vaults who never show emotion and never have pedestrian needs like sleep or food.

And I had done exactly what they'd asked of me. I'd been taking calls with China while I was in labor–right before they wheeled me into the OR for my c-section. And I'd come back after only a few weeks, pumping breast milk in my office in the middle of the night after I put them to bed.

So many years, so much of myself given, just to have it all taken away from me.

Just so Rick–the sentient golf club with a receding hairline–could make partner instead of me? I'm not even sure he can spell litigation, yet here he is, the newest partner.

Be perfect. Be in control. It had been ingrained in me my entire life. And I was shaking and cracking, and the explosion was imminent.

And then there was the house. My great-aunt Louise, God bless her, always supported me, and she had left me her most valuable asset. Her house, a 5,000-square-foot brownstone in Boston's historic South End. The kind of jaw-dropping real estate that makes investors faint and is my dream house. Aunt Louise knew I always wanted to move into that brownstone.

But there was just one problem . . .

Since the money had run out over a decade ago, there hadn't been much happening in the way of maintenance or repairs. Add to that the fact that Aunt Louise lived in a nursing home for most of her final years and, well, the house is a bit of a mess.

Without my law firm salary, there is no way I can make the mortgage on my Beacon Hill townhouse, pay the girls' school tuition, help my mom out, and pay for the brownstone repairs. The sensible thing would be just to sell the brownstone but I can't let go of my dream house. Not with everything else I've lost.

I was well paid but after my dramatic exit, I will need to sell the townhouse to fix the falling down brownstone. Too bad it needs so much work because living in it as is will not be fun. Just another source of panic to add to my crazy plate.

And I had so wanted to be present this weekend. To have fun with my friends and enjoy this special ritual we've carved out for ourselves. The space and time to connect and be the people we were before jobs and kids and responsibility had drained the life out of us.

So, with my Yeti filled with wine, I walk down the beach. Becket might be a controlling jerkface, but he has excellent booze. I'm going to drink it, stare at the ocean, and try to figure my life out.

I walk down the beach toward he jetty in the distance. The closer I get the more the rocks glisten in the moonlight. Once I step onto the jetty, I kick a rock with my sandaled foot but it hardly moves.

I pick it up, letting it roll around in my hand, feeling the weight of it.

And then I throw it, far and hard, watching as it splashes into the ocean with a satisfying *plop*. Fuck, that felt good.

I grab another, slightly larger, and throw it.

I walk along the water's edge, picking up the loose rocks that had, at one time, been part of the structure, and hurl each one as hard as I can.

Some require two hands and don't go far, while others sail into the surf. Throwing a particularly big one, I get hit with the backsplash.

"Fuck!"

I had discarded my sandals and am half-soaked at this

point. I snag a nail on a big one, bemoaning the fact that regular manicures are probably no longer a part of my life.

A year ago, I was a successful partner-track lawyer with adorable gifted twins.

Now I was an unemployed train wreck, soon I'll be living in a condemned building filled with vermin and no doubt, a few ghosts. And my kids have developed into supervillains seemingly overnight.

When did everything go so far off the rails?

All these years I swore I could do it all, but right now . . . I know I can't.

"Are you trying to murder a sea turtle?"

I turn and see Dylan standing on the beach, her long auburn curls blowing softly in the breeze. Damn her and her tranquility.

"Maybe," I say nonchalantly, picking up another rock. Sadly my cool act is ruined when my bare foot snags on a loose rock, sending me stumbling. I haven't even made a dent in that wine yet.

"That's why I don't believe in shoes," Dylan murmurs dreamily, picking up a rock and studying it like it possesses hot stock tips. "You have to feel the rocks, absorb their energy and let it meld with yours. Let them feel your fire."

I stand, blinking at my friend. After almost two decades, I still have no idea what the fuck she's talking about most of the time. So instead I chose another rock, bigger this time.

"Do you want help with that? It's pretty big."

I nod.

She walks over and bends to grab the other side of the boulder. Together, we get it up.

"Okay. We throw on three."

We rock back, shifting the weight. "One, two, three." And

we let it go, sailing probably five or six feet before plunking into the water, sending foamy spray at us.

"I like how you're attempting to rebalance your chakras," Dylan says, tucking a wisp of hair behind her ear, displaying a row of piercings. "But I find meditation is usually more effective–and it doesn't cause coastal erosion–but if your soul is craving heavy work, who am I to argue?"

I look at her and smile. "Sorry. I'm just working some shit out." I flick my gaze back in the direction of the house. "What are you doing up so late?" It was past midnight, and I assumed everyone was passed out for the night. One of the benefits of traveling without kids, uninterrupted sleep.

"Sleep and I are not close friends, and the stars are the best part of the day. I was taking a walk and found someone violently assaulting the ocean. Mother Gaia is concerned. She's going to have a conversation with Poseidon, Neptune, and Kanaloa about what to do with you. And we all know that won't go well . . ."

I do not know what she means but whatever she's talking about, I know it comes from a place of concern and kindness, so I love her anyway.

I pick up my shoes and walk back toward the house, kicking the water as I go. "My life is fucked."

"Then I think rock throwing is probably necessary and healing. But maybe take a moment to reflect? Here. Grab another rock and try this."

Willing to listen to her hippie shit for just another minute, I bend down and pick up another rock. Its medium sized and has one jagged edge, big enough to break a window but not big enough to dislocate my shoulder trying to throw it.

"Close your eyes and channel your fears and anger into the rock, into every microscopic piece of sand and salt and earth within it. The negativity in your soul is snuffing out all your beautiful colors. You need to channel that dark energy and cast it away into the abyss."

"Fuck everything," I whisper, throwing the rock.

"Good one. Now to really cleanse yourself, you should probably say the problem out loud. Make sure the universe can hear it."

I shrug, putting my wine down to help me get a better grip. The next rock sails farther before dropping with a satisfying *plunk*. "I fucked up my career," I yell, "and now I'm unemployed."

She hands me another one. "Louder."

"I worry I can't provide for my family."

Plop.

Maybe Dylan was right. Because big, fat tears are streaming down my cheeks.

My vision is blurred, but I set my sights on an even bigger rock.

"I'm just not good enough," I yell, attempting to throw the big one and then drop into the sand, the waves licking at my feet.

Dylan holds out a hand to me. "You're not done yet. You're not fully cleansed. You've got to get it all out. Say all the unsayable things."

It isn't often that Dylan makes sense, but in this moment, she seems almost prophetic.

I stand back up and retrieve the next rock.

"Make sure to yell," she says, encouraging me.

I hurl it, grunting loudly and shouting, "I take care of everyone, and no one takes care of me! I push myself day in and day out and it's never enough! I'm alone on this goddamn earth, and it sucks donkey balls."

And then I collapse. All the muscles in my body ache and the tears just keep flowing.

Dylan sits next to me, her long skirt getting wet. She pulls me close and sits with me as I cry. "It's all going to be okay," she whispers as she pats my head.

"Yeah?" I sniffle. "Says who?"

She gives me a soft smile. "The universe."

Dylan

Of the three women sitting around the beach fire, I can't decide who is the most tense. Stressing out on the beautiful beach under a million stars? Like how is that even possible when life has given us this amazing trip. But tight smiles, white-knuckled grips on the wineglasses, and life-changing secrets mean I need to do something. The big kind of something so they'll get out of their own heads. But watching them through the large kitchen windows, I'm not sure exactly what.

I love these three women like they are my sisters–and the good kind of siblings, not the kind parents should put up for adoption. But man, I will not make it through life if I carry worries the way Liv, Delia, and Shay do.

Sometimes they need to breathe in, breathe out. Meditate on it. Adding more time for yoga will help them. Despite my ridiculous number of reminders, 'chilllax' is not my best friends' favorite word.

"Who the hell keeps doing these?" Beckett huffs from the library. All weekend the grumpy gazillionaire has been annoyed that the random puzzles in the library were getting done every few hours, especially since no one claims to be doing them.

I move to the edge of the door to spy on him. I hold back my chuckle, watching the large man jump over one of the thirteen puzzles littering the floor so he can get to his desk.

"I keep telling you it's me, and for that matter, young man, stop picking on that lovely brunette. I'll never get great grandchildren if you don't learn the right way to treat wonderful women–and don't give me that 'she's my employee' shit." The high-pitched voice echoes around the library as I silently head back to the wine fridge to grab two bottles. I plan to get my friends wasted.

"The fuck is that voice?" Beckett stomps into the room, his brown eyes narrowing when he sees me. "Stop doing that, hippy dippy do." He's been calling me that all week. It's supposed to annoy me, but I think the universe is giving him a lesson about patience through me, so I don't mind. "I know you're some kind of ventriloquist."

Even though he's told me twice that his grandmother hasn't passed away yet, I've been pretending to be her ghost for the last three days. I tip my head and bat my lashes. "Venn . . . what?"

He points what is meant to be a threatening finger at me. "You're nutty, but not dumb. You know exactly what I mean."

"Do I, Beck?" I ask as I open a large bottle of expensive red wine. At least I assume it's expensive because everything about Liv's boss is over the top.

"Beckett."

"No." I move to the second bottle. "Your name is Beck, people who want to kiss your ass add the extra 'it' to make you feel important."

"I—" He blinks. "I'm not even sure what the fuck you're saying."

Well, that makes two of us. Sometimes my mouth just opens and words come out; I roll with them because, really, what else can I do?

"Why are you still in a suit when you're on vacation?" The man hasn't even loosened his tie, even though it's past nine at night. The stick that lives up Beckett's ass is so high; he should worry it might poke him in the eye one day. Another person who needs to learn the meaning of *chill*.

He glares at me one more time before pushing off the large island, heading for the door leading to my friends. Messing with Beckett has been fun all weekend, but I have limits and tonight my friends, especially Liv, need a break, and Beckett is going to make the muck of her life muckier.

I round the island and stop between him and the door. "No."

"No?" he deadpans.

"Do you not see all the gray and black in the air out there?" Those poor women's auras are all dark and gloomy. It's sad because normally, they shine bright pink, purple, green, blue, even some white. But tonight, negativity mixes with the energy all around them.

"Are you talking about the *smoke* from the *fire*?" His brow rises as his lips turn down. He's so blind.

"No. Stop looking with your eyes and start seeing with your heart." I toss my arms up in the air and move back to the bottles on the counter. "They need some space to drink wine and just *be*."

Beckett rubs his temples with his fingertips brushing his dark hair. "You know what, I can't with you. You win. I'll let Liv be tonight. Just make sure she's ready to work tomorrow."

"She'll be the perfect amount of hungover." I point my blue

fingernail at the ceiling, trying to mimic the Boy Scout pledge, but I never paid attention to the details of it when my thirteen-year-old had done Scouts.

Beckett doesn't look impressed, so I'm not sure I hit the mark. Did I accidentally do the gang sign for the guys who run around Newark? Hmm. Maybe.

"Good night, dippy do."

"Night, Bec."

He growls, but I certainly will never be enough of a kiss-ass to use his full name again. I brush my long hair over my shoulder so it won't get into the wine bottles before I pick them both up. My friends will never know the buzzkill I saved them from, but that's okay; I know they're thanking me, anyway.

As I leave the house, the only sounds I hear are from the lapping of the waves on the white-sand beach and the crackle of the fire. It's a fairly big island. Beckett's house is the only one on here, but there is a ton of staff. They seem to magically appear like Voldemort's minions when someone needs something and fade into the black when they don't. So the entire place is quiet.

Quiet, peaceful, and beautiful.

"I swear, Dyl, you float when you walk, you never make a single sound."

It's probably more likely that Shay's so worried about something and she isn't paying attention, but it would be wild if I did actually float. How many people can do something like that?

"You know what else is crazy? How like the ocean always makes waves," I say as I drop into the only empty chair around the fire pit. I hand a bottle of merlot to Liv, who fills her and Shay's glasses with the burgundy goodness. "Rocks, or boats, or even this island don't get in its way, it just makes the waves."

Three sets of confused eyes inform me I'm not making

sense, so I go in a different direction. "Liam got expelled from school."

"What?" Delia exclaims.

Liv chokes on her wine, coughing as she pounds herself on the chest. Even hacking on her drink, she's cute. The girl-next-door kind of adorable, with big brown eyes and the kind of curves I have spent my life wishing for.

"Did the school really just call you?" Shay lifts her hand, running it through her short black hair.

I wave them off. "Oh no, this happened two months ago." I thought I'd told someone, but the wide-eyed shock from all three proves I didn't. This works out better, as if life knew this moment was coming and that's why I'd never mentioned it.

"It was a thing, and ya know, it's not hard to be a shithead when you're thirteen." Not being in that school anymore has been great for him. It was meant to be.

Liv reaches for my glass and fills it to the top. "Why didn't you tell us? Maybe we could have helped?"

"Yes." Delia slams her wine on the armrest of her Adirondack chair. It sloshes over the rim and droplets shoot up, but luckily, they miss her pink off-the-shoulder T-shirt. "Was it legal for the school to expel him? Maybe we need to sue them."

That's something I hadn't considered, but it's irrelevant because I'm home-schooling him and he works at my preschool–and both are doing wonders for him. He's happier.

"Social interaction is important for general health. Has Liam been getting enough?" Shay's brow crease, marring her otherwise flawless skin. "I'd also recommend lavender and chamomile tea, or potentially removing gluten from his diet."

"He's doing good, so let's not sue anyone this week." I shake my head at the idea of all that stress. *Ugh, that sounds gross.* "I'm pretty sure it's not a gluten allergy, either." Life would suck without bagels. "It's more like the world decided he needed a new road, but it had to make a big mess of the area before a clear path was paved."

Liv cocks her head and wisps of brown hair fall out of her bun into her eyes. She bats them away. "But why didn't you tell us?"

I look at her pointedly. "Sometimes it's hard sharing news that makes you feel like a failure." My eyes linger on Liv until she glances at the sand. Then I switch to Shay, who looks over my head. And lastly Delia, who finds the water super interesting. "Anyone else ever feel that way?"

My gaze lands on Liv because she'll be the first to crack. She blows out a hard breath, making her lips vibrate against each other.

"I'm getting a divorce because Drake had an affair with our nanny." Her entire body slumps into the chair with the weight that came off her by telling us.

Both Shay and Delia ask rapid-fire questions, but no one's shocked. Drake is a douche, so even if divorce is horrible, we all know Liv is better off without him.

"My final straw wasn't even the affair." Liv takes a huge gulp of wine after making the admission. "It was shaming Finn for wearing a dress."

The story hits me less like a wrecking ball because I've heard it, but Delia and Shay are ready to torch the man.

"Why didn't you tell us?" Shay asks. Liv hands her the half-empty bottle, and she fills Delia's glass with more wine.

I raise an eyebrow at her. "Hard to admit when life sucks, right? No matter how much your friends want to support you."

Shay swallows a fortifying sip of wine. "I've been struggling with single parenting since Ajay died. I feel like I'm worried about Kai every second of every day, and I don't have time for anything or anyone else, including myself. It's so hard. I have no idea how you two do the single parent thing." Her charcoal-colored eyes cut from Delia to me.

"I never could have survived those first few years without you all," I reply. I had Liam when I was still in college. He'd been a surprise and these three women were my support system. It's easy to see that it's my time to return the favor to all of them. They need me, and I'll figure out a plan. I just need the universe to start talking and point me in the right direction.

"I didn't know you were having a hard time, Shay!" Delia reaches out and grabs her arm.

"Me either," Liv admits.

"It's just a lot, and I don't have the support in California. But I don't know where else to go, either." Shay shrugs. "I felt ridiculous telling you guys that even after two years, I'm still struggling."

"Never feel that way. We want to help," Delia assures, but my stare is now on her.

"Because we should all know when one of us has issues, right?" I ask pointedly.

She sighs, getting the gist of what I'm asking, and leans back, letting her blond bun rest against the top of the white chair. "Fine. I'm going to have to sell my town house and move into my dream house that my aunt left me, but it's falling down. And the twins are a lot. On top of that, I didn't make partner, so I impulse-quit the second the announcement was made. I'm an unemployed single mother of double-trouble twins with an enormous house that's falling down and I don't know if I have enough money to fix it. So, you know . . . just living the dream."

I sit back, letting the three women finally unload to each other what they already admitted to me. Specifically, that perfect isn't a thing and we're all struggling. They refill their glasses and honestly talk for the first time this weekend. And after it's all out, the air feels lighter. Like all that gray haze hovering around them has lifted, allowing their gorgeous rainbow of colors to shine again.

"This mess with Drake seems less huge after talking with you three." Liv finishes off her third, or maybe it's her fourth, refill.

She wobbles just slightly in her seat. I may have lied about how hungover she'll be tomorrow.

Shay giggles. "Nothing about Drake is huge." She might be more drunk than Liv, especially considering her weight loss over the last year. She's always been tiny, five-foot-nothing and thin, but her obsession with healthy living has her even thinner these days. It's surprising she hasn't banned alcohol from her body, though she did request organic wine with a lower glycemic index. Hmm, I think I forgot to check the wine I brought out . . . Oh well.

"It does help to unload on each other. I wish you two lived closer." Delia sighs. Both she and Liv still live in the Boston area where we went to school. I'd moved by my older brother in Jersey, and Shay had gone back to her home state of California. But Delia is right; closer would be nice. But before anyone can get bummed over our distance, I step in.

"While we're all still together, this is what we need to do." I stand and yank my white tank top over my head.

"I'm not going skinny-dipping." Shay wedges her glass in the sand and crosses her arms. "People drown at night in the ocean. Plus, salt water can damage your hair cuticles."

"No one is going in the water." We definitely need to hang out more so she'll remember life isn't always scary, that she can't always be wound up so tight. "What we all need to do is unload our burdens and toss them into the fire. So, take your shirts off and throw them in, letting our fears burn away." I spin my tank top over my head.

"I can't do that!" Liv exclaims. "I'm on my boss's property!"

I roll my eyes. "Bec's red turns a hell of a lot of orange around you. And I've watched him stare at your chest. Trust me, he won't mind." I'm not sure if either Liv or Beckett realize the charged sexual energy floating in the air whenever they're together. The orange glow around both of them is fierce.

A blush rises up Liv's cheeks. "He does *not*. His aura stays perfectly red all the time."

Shay and Delia laugh. They know I'm right. I ignore Liv's protests, but the fact that she's talking auras means she's totally deflecting. I spin my shirt a few more times before tossing it into the crackling orange flames. "I'm a good mom, and my kid will be okay, even if our life's not traditional and I refuse to let myself think anything else."

I turn to my left and raise an eyebrow at Shay.

She pulls off her navy T-shirt, revealing the string of butterflies tattooed on her bicep. "I can single-parent and sleep, even if it's hard. I'll just have to buy more–" she clears her throat. "toys to help me with the latter."

Her shirt hits the fire and I stare down Delia.

She inches up her pink shirt, pausing before finally yanking it off. "I can parent alone, fix a house, and figure out a new career." She tosses her shirt in with a sigh. "Wow, I'm a hot mess."

Tall, blond, and beautiful, men always stare at her, so there's no question about the hot.

"We're burning the negative. You're not a mess; life is just teaching you to embrace the chaos."

Delia chuckles. "I think you've been teaching me that for fifteen years, but I will try to embrace the positives, like being with my best friends."

"Fuck it." Finally, Liv lifts her T-shirt over her head. She looks toward Beckett's villa as if she'll catch him spying on her. Wouldn't surprise me–the man watches her like he wants her for a snack. "I can make it through divorce and come out better."

"And now . . ." I hit the button on my phone, "we dance." Taylor Swift blasts into the air, and my best friends and I shake our booties like we used to back in college. Ironically, we used to be under-clad and uncoordinated then, too, like ducks around a hot pole.

It's only a few minutes of giggles before a chill shoots up my spine.

Oh my God, I've got it.

I stop the music.

"The universe gave us the answer like I knew it would." I smile at them. "The plan is so freaking clear now that the negative juju is gone, we can see it."

Delia's thin brows rise as Liv shakes her head. Shay turns in a circle, trying to see what I might be referring to. I guess they can't see it yet.

"What plan?" Shay sounds worried.

"We all move into Delia's house together!" I clap my hands, giving them my brightest smile. "We fix it up, raise our kids, and support each other. We'll mom-com this shit up!"

"Mom-com?" Liv frowns.

"Yeah, mom community." I smile. "How *fun* will that be?"

WANT MORE MOM COMS?

PREORDER ON AMAZON

ABOUT BRITTANEE NICOLE

Brittanee is an author who lives in New England with her husband and two children. Her town is a character in itself in all of her books. When she is not writing she enjoys spending time outdoors by the water with her children, reading at the beach or by the pool (or really anywhere), dancing with her friends, singing Karaoke, spinning, bike riding and boating.

ABOUT JENNI BARA

Jenni Bara lives in New Jersey working as a paralegal in family law, writing real-life unhappily ever-afters every day. In turn, she spends her free time with anything that keeps her laughing, including life with kids. She loves writing books with a great balance of life, love, and laughter.

ABOUT SWATI M.H.

Swati MH is a Texas raised contemporary romance author living in the Bay Area with her very own book husband and two beautiful daughters. When she's not writing stories full of humor, heart, and heartbreak, she's likely thinking about doing so . . . preferably while holding a glass of wine.

ABOUT DAPHNE ELLIOT

In High School, Daphne Elliot was voted "most likely to become a romance novelist." After spending the last decade as a corporate lawyer, she has finally embraced her destiny. Her small town steamy novels are filled with flirty banter, sexy hijinks, and lots and lots of heart.